SILVERHEELS™

by
Bruce Jones
Scott Hampton
&
April Campbell

Silverheels

First printing, July, 1987

Published by Eclipse Books, P.O. Box 1099, Forestville, California 95436

Trade paperback: ISBN 0-913035-22-X Hardcover: ISBN 0-913035-26-2 Limited Edition hardcover: ISBN 0-913035-27-0

DEDICATION

To Gloria and Wade Hampton,
my mom and dad.
With love,
Scott Hampton,
January, 1987

Chapter 1

MY LIFE IS ON THIS COMPOUND; I KNOW NO OTHER. HERE I HUNT RABBIJACKS, SLEEP ON THE DIRT BENEATH THE BLOODY MOON. THE BARRIER ENCLOSES US, STANDING AS IT HAS STOOD SINCE BEFORE MY GRANDFERE WAS BORN, AND ROUND ITS FRINGES ARE STAKED PALE NAZITE GUARDS, PROTECTING THEIR WORLD FROM THE LIKES OF ***US***...

IN THE DISTANCE I SEE THE CITY OF LIGHTS. ABOVE IT HOVERS AN AMBER FOG, AND BENEATH THAT FOG LIVE THE NAZITES: OUR KEEPERS. BY DAY I CANNOT REACH THEM, MY WORLDLY BODY STAYS TRAPPED BY THIS PRISON OF WIRE MESH, BUT BY NIGHT!--BY NIGHT I AM THE ***DREAMER!*** MY SOUL FLIES THROUGH THE COMPOUND BARRIER AND TRAVELS INTO THAT CITY, INTO THE SLEEK AEROFARES AND LOFTY TOWERS, THROUGH THE AQUADUCTS, OVER THE MILITARY INSTALLATION, WHERE THE NIGHTFLIERS MARCH FORMATION BENEATH THAT AMBER FIRMAMENT. THE NAZITES SLEEP AND I ENTER THEIR MINDS, THE WAY I ENTER THE MIND OF THE RABBIJACK AS I STALK IT; I SEE THEIR PASTS AND FUTURES, I SENSE THEIR FEARS...

GRANDFERE SAYS MY TALENT WAS BORN OF THE RAINING WAR, WHEN BLOOD AND FIRE RAN FROM THE SKIES. I AM THE FIRST DREAMER MY TRIBE HAS KNOWN. I AM...

FORTY SEASONS AGO I WAS BORN TO THIS COMPOUND. MY MOTHER DID NOT SURVIVE MY BIRTH...

...BUT MY GRANDFERE RAISED ME UP WELL, SHOWING ME THE WAYS OF OUR PEOPLE, THE 'PACHEES...
SEE, CHILD? THE STICK SMELLS THE WATER BENEATH THE EARTH! WE SHALL DIG HERE!

MY INSTINCT TO SURVIVE WAS STRONG. I LEARNED WELL...
SILVERHEELS, BEWARE!
AH! WE SHALL FEAST TONIGHT!

I WAS FASTEST, SUREST, THE MOST CUNNING BRAVE IN THE TRIBE...I WAS THE MOST ALONE...

THEY HATE ME, GRANDFERE...
THEY FEAR YOU, SILVERHEELS. THEY BELIEVE YOU ARE POSSESSED. THEY DO NOT UNDERSTAND YOUR GREAT GIFT!
...BUT I DO, MY SON...

GRANDFERE IS TIMEKEEPER AND WEAVER OF TALES. HE KEEPS THE HISTORY OF OUR TRIBE IN HIS HEART...
ONCE THE RED 'PACHEE ROAMED FREE IN THE OUTWORLD, LONG BEFORE THE NAZITE ROSE TO POWER...

"THE NAZITE SENT THE 'PACHEE AND ALL MEN OF COLOR TO DIE IN THE COMPOUNDS, AND SET OUT TO CONQUER THE STARS..."

"BUT THE STARS FOUGHT BACK!..."

AND WERE THE NAZITES DEFEATED?
OH, NO, LITTLE ONE, ONLY DRIVEN BACK! THE NAZITES ARE GODS! THEY ARE INVINCIBLE!

BUT GRANDFERE IS WRONG... I KNOW THEM TO BE MERELY MEN...

THE CITY OF LIGHTS GLEAMS WITH CIVILIZATION; IN THE COMPOUND LIFE IS SAVAGE...

A MAN MUST BE SWIFT AND CRUEL TO SURVIVE. A MAN MUST BE AN ANIMAL...

NO GAME IS TOO QUICK OR CLEVER FOR ME--I KNOW WHAT'S IN ITS MIND!...

THERE HE IS, THE DEVIL! HE'S MURDERED MY SISTER CHIALA! AFTER HIM!

YOU CALL YOURSELF DREAMER! HERE IS A DREAM FOR YOU, DEMON!

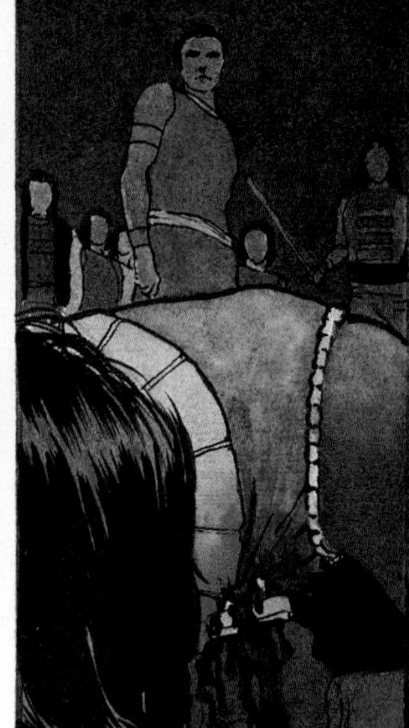

SILVERHEELS, RUN! THEY MEAN TO DESTROY YOU!
CHIALA, DEAD! BUT WHO COULD HAVE DONE SUCH A THING?...
FROM THE CITY OF LIGHTS SHOOTS A SILVER ROCKET! HOW I WISH I WERE UPON IT!

AND FROM THE DARKNESS COMES THE ANSWER TO MY QUESTION...
YOU LIKE THE ROCKET, JA? BEAUTIFUL, IS IT NOT?

AUNWOOD, THE NIGHT GUARD! HIS SKIN IS WHITE AS MAGGOT'S FLESH--IN HIS BLACK MIND FESTERS A LUST FOR RED WOMEN--A LUST HE HAS SATISFIED THIS NIGHT!
VERY PRETTY ROCKET, PIG MAN. TOO PRETTY FOR YOUR KIND...

PERHAPS I BLIND YOU, SO YOU NEVER SEE THAT ROCKET AGAIN! JA? PERHAPS A LESSON...
ZZTTTTT!
HA-HA-HA!
ZZTTT!
ZZTTT!
ZZTTT!
HA-HA-HA! FILTHY RED!
ZZTTT!
ZZTTT!

...MAKE REPAIRS TOMORROW...BEFORE INSPECTION...

DEATH LIES BEFORE ME AND BEHIND. I CANNOT GO FORWARD OR BACK; I CAN ONLY SLEEP--

--AND DREAM...

THE MOMENT MY EYES CLOSE, MY SOUL IS GONE! THROUGH THE BARRIER, OVER AUNWOOD, INTO THE CITY OF LIGHTS...

IT IS MORE THAN AN ENTERTAINMENT, THIS DREAMING--IT IS MY LIFE! I EXIST ONLY WHEN I DREAM...
FUHRSTAUGEN MILITARY INSTALLATION

I SEE THE LIGHT IN THE GENERAL'S CONFERENCE ROOM--A SECRET MEETING!

--CHAIRMAN OF THE INTERGALLACTIC COUNCIL WILL ARRIVE AT THE FIRST MORNING'S LIGHT. HE SHALL CHOOSE CANDIDATES TO REPRESENT EARTH ON THE LAWKEEPERS' FORCE. OUR BEST CADETS WILL VIE FOR THE POST. IT IS A GREAT HONOR--
...AND THE SECRETS OF THE CIVILIZED ARE ALWAYS INTERESTING.
HONOR, BAH! THE COUNCIL HATES US! THIS IS JUST ANOTHER WAY TO PROLONG OUR PROBATION UNTIL WE PROVE WE WILL NOT WAGE WAR AGAIN!

MAJOR ROSCH, WE HAVE MET THE TERMS OF PROBATION. WE HAVE ABOLISHED AGGRESSIVE BEHAVIOR, PIRACY, SLAVERY--
BUT THE COMPOUNDS!
THE COUNCIL KNOWS NOTHING OF THE COMPOUNDS! WE CHART THEM AS GAME RESERVES!

WITH OUR MAN ON THE INTERGALLACTIC LAW-KEEPERS' FORCE, THE COUNCIL WILL GROW MORE TRUSTING, LESS CAUTIOUS. OUR MAN WILL PROVE VERY USEFUL... STEPAN, IF YOU PLEASE...
CADET STEPAN KRAUS WILL BE OUR MAN ON THE FORCE. IT HAS BEEN ARRANGED...
NO!

GRANDFERE!
SILVERHEELS! ARE YOU THERE?
I'VE SEARCHED ALL NIGHT FOR YOU, MY SON!

LISTEN, OLD MAN! I'M LEAVING THE COMPOUND!
BUT--BUT TO LEAVE IS TO DIE!
I'M DEAD ALREADY!!

WHAT'S THE USE! YOU'LL NEVER UNDER-STAND--YOU'RE AS DEAD AS I!
SILVERHEELS, WAIT!

AUNWOOD!
WHAT? WHO IS THERE...

AUNWOOD!
ROTH, IS THAT YOU? COME TO REPLACE MY WATCH SO EARLY, MY FRIEND?

R-ROTH?

AAAAAAGGH!
KRK-KRK
KKRAAACKACK!!

FOR MURDERING CHIALA, "PIG-MAN"...

THEY'RE COMING! PAPA, LOOK!
HUSH, MIRANDA! I SEE IT! YOU'RE MAKING A SPECTACLE OF YOURSELF!
IT'S SO EXCITING! ALIENS!
REPULSIVE IS WHAT THEY ARE! DISGUSTING! INFERIORS!
BUT THEY'VE BEATEN US TO OUR KNEES, HAVEN'T THEY, FATHER?
WE WILL SEE...
MR. CHAIRMAN, AN HONOR! WE GREET THE INTERGALLACTIC COUNCIL MOST HUMBLY!
LAST TIME WE MET YOU CALLED ME 'SWINE'. BUT THAT IS LONG AGO AND FORGOTTEN, IS IT NOT, GENERAL?
ER--YES, MR. CHAIRMAN...
MAY I PRESENT MY DAUGHTER MIRANDA?
AH, YES--YOU HAVE ARRANGED FOR HER TO ACCOMPANY YOU ON THE TRAINING MISSION. CHARMED, MY DEAR.
A... PLEASURE, MR. CHAIRMAN...

HERE ARE THE CADETS, MR. CHAIRMAN, IF YOU'LL STEP THIS WAY...
...GOOD...VERY GOOD...
...REINHART... STEPPEL...FEDDERS ...JOFFEE...
--AND THIS IS CADET STEPAN KRAUS--
STOP! STOP HIM! YOU CAN'T GO THERE!
LET-- GO!
BRING HIM FORWARD!
AND WHO MIGHT YOU BE, YOUNG NAZITE?
NAZITE? HE'S NO NAZITE, HE'S--
--CADET SILVERHEELS, SIR, REPORTING FOR DUTY!
I WANT TO BECOME A LAWKEEPER!
B-BUT--H-HE'S NOT QUALIFIED, HE--
NO, GENERAL, YOU'RE WRONG. HE'S AN EXCELLENT REPRESENTATIVE OF YOUR PLANET, A FINE SPECIMEN! I THINK HE WILL COMPETE ADMIRABLY!
BUT-- BUT--

SERGEANT GOLU!
SIR?
BRING THE CADETS ABOARD. WE LEAVE AT ONCE!
YES, SIR!

GENERAL? YOUR LUGGAGE IS ABOARD. ARE YOU AND YOUR DAUGHTER READY TO LEAVE?
MIRANDA, I THINK YOU SHOULD--
I'M GOING, FATHER! I WANT TO GO! DON'T TRY TO CHANGE MY MIND!

THEN COME!

ALL RIGHT, CADETS. RIGHT FACE.

FORWARD-- MARCH!

FOOL! COWARD! YOU SHOULD HAVE SAVED YOUR PEOPLE! YOU'LL NEVER SAVE YOURSELF!

YOU'RE A DEAD MAN, SILVERHEELS...

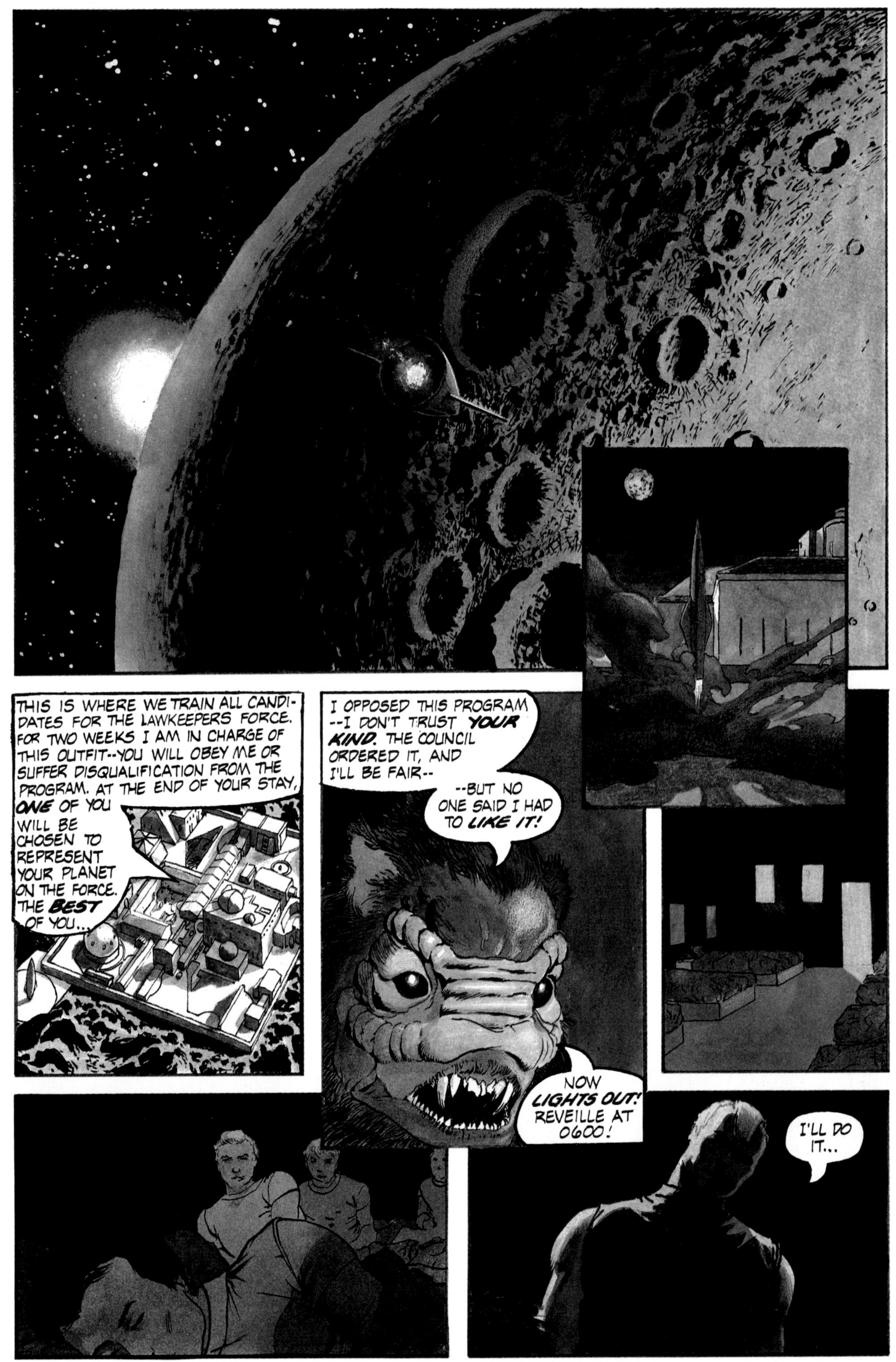
THIS IS WHERE WE TRAIN ALL CANDIDATES FOR THE LAWKEEPERS FORCE. FOR TWO WEEKS I AM IN CHARGE OF THIS OUTFIT--YOU WILL OBEY ME OR SUFFER DISQUALIFICATION FROM THE PROGRAM. AT THE END OF YOUR STAY, ONE OF YOU WILL BE CHOSEN TO REPRESENT YOUR PLANET ON THE FORCE. THE BEST OF YOU...
I OPPOSED THIS PROGRAM --I DON'T TRUST YOUR KIND. THE COUNCIL ORDERED IT, AND I'LL BE FAIR--
--BUT NO ONE SAID I HAD TO LIKE IT!
NOW LIGHTS OUT! REVEILLE AT 0600!
I'LL DO IT...

--FILTHY SAVAGE--STARING AT MY MIRANDA, MY FIANCEE--ONE THING ON YOUR DIRTY RED MIND--
AAGH!
CRUSH HIM, STEPAN!
KILL HIM!

ENOUGH!

KRAUS, SILVERHEELS, CLEAN UP! THE REST OF YOU, IN YOUR BUNKS! ONE MORE DISPLAY LIKE THIS AND THE PROGRAM IS CANCELLED!
FOR ALL OF YOU!

--JUST WAIT--

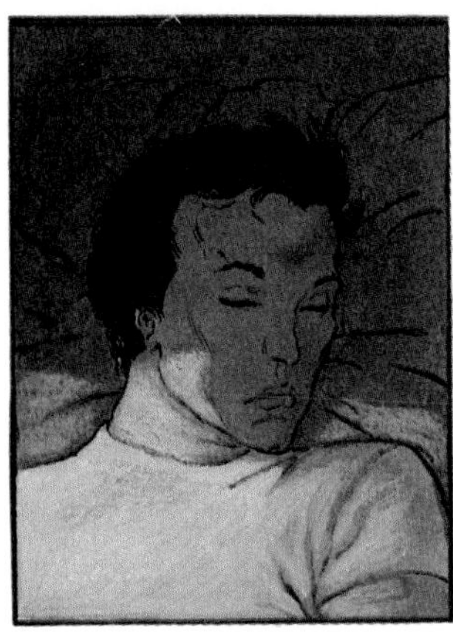

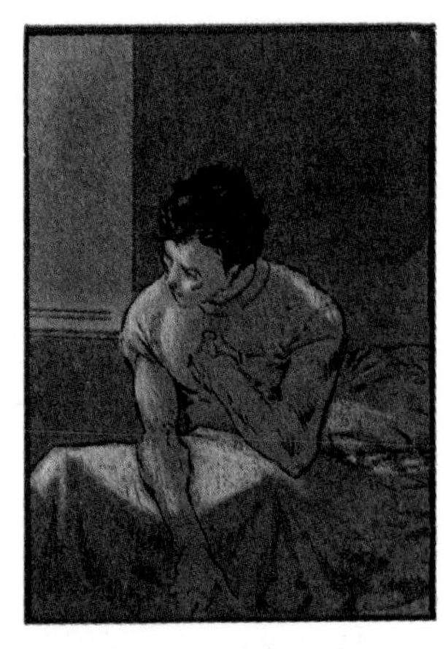

YOU'VE COME AT LAST!

YOU--DON'T HATE ME...
ON THE CONTRARY-- I'VE BEEN WAITING FOR YOU--
--ALL MY LIFE!

Chapter 2

DAY ONE...
ALL RIGHT, YOU LAZY MAGGOTS! UP AND DRESSED!

JUST WAIT, LITTLE RED...

MOVE IT!

FALL IN!

WHERE CAN THEY BE GOING? IT'S BARELY DAWN!

MIRANDA, COME BACK HERE! YOU'RE NOT EVEN DRESSED!

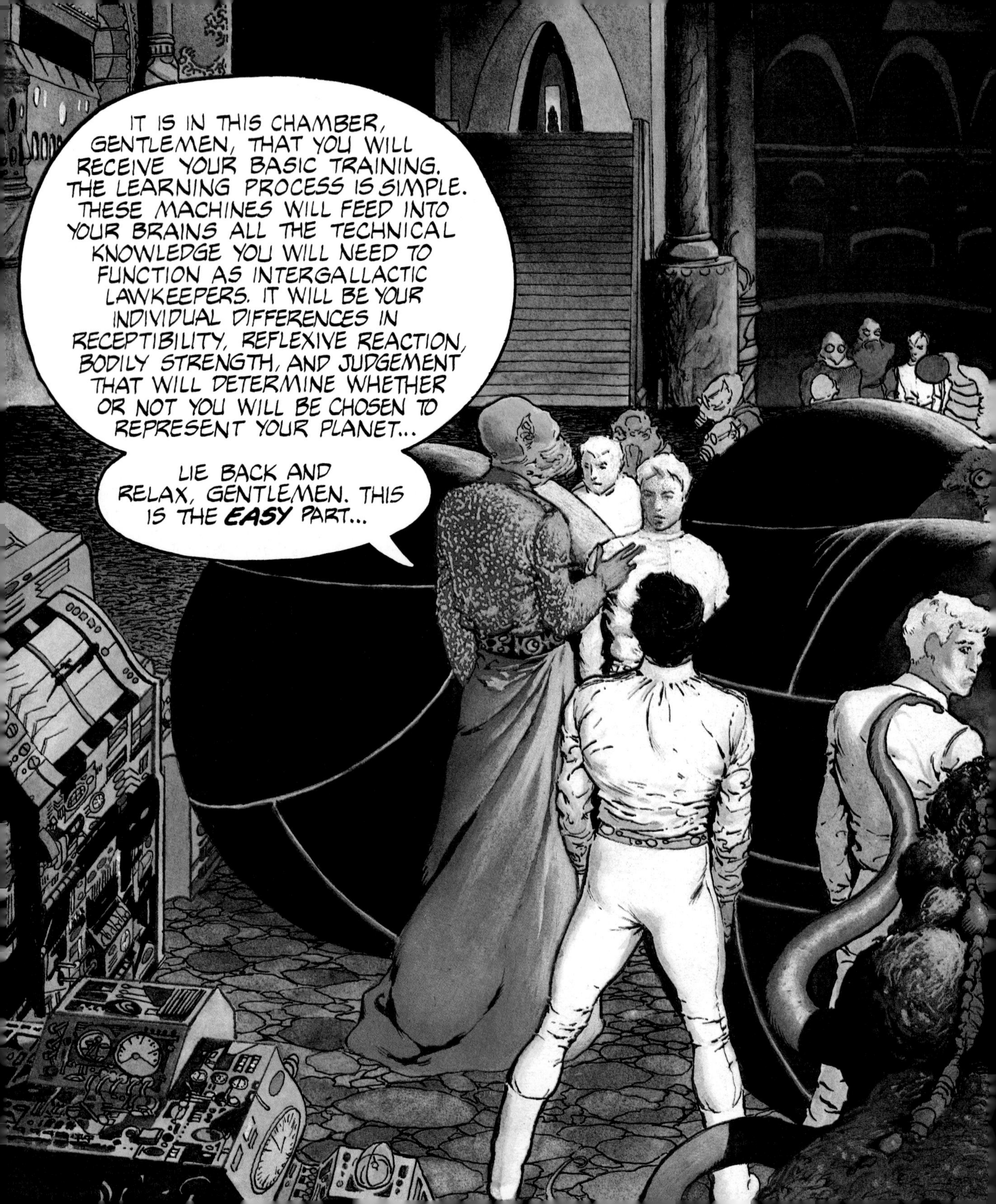
IT IS IN THIS CHAMBER, GENTLEMEN, THAT YOU WILL RECEIVE YOUR BASIC TRAINING. THE LEARNING PROCESS IS SIMPLE. THESE MACHINES WILL FEED INTO YOUR BRAINS ALL THE TECHNICAL KNOWLEDGE YOU WILL NEED TO FUNCTION AS INTERGALLACTIC LAWKEEPERS. IT WILL BE YOUR INDIVIDUAL DIFFERENCES IN RECEPTIBILITY, REFLEXIVE REACTION, BODILY STRENGTH, AND JUDGEMENT THAT WILL DETERMINE WHETHER OR NOT YOU WILL BE CHOSEN TO REPRESENT YOUR PLANET...
LIE BACK AND RELAX, GENTLEMEN. THIS IS THE ***EASY*** PART...

ALL RIGHT, CADETS, NOW--

HEY! YOU CAN'T COME IN HERE! NO WOMEN ALLOWED!

NONSENSE, SERGEANT! WE'VE TRAINED MANY WOMEN IN THESE CHAMBERS!
COME IN, MY DEAR...

BUT, SIR, SHE'S NOT EVEN A CADET! SHE'LL DISTRACT THE MEN--
THAT'S ENOUGH, SERGEANT. SHE'S THE GENERAL'S DAUGHTER AND OUR HONORED GUEST, AND I WANT YOU TO SHOW THE YOUNG LADY EVERY RESPECT.
YES, SIR...

TAKE A SEAT, THEN. AND YOU MEN, LIE BACK AND QUIT GAWKING! WE HAVEN'T GOT ALL BLOODY DAY!

HERE ...WE... GO!

DOES IT HURT THEM?
OF COURSE NOT, MY DEAR. A PAINLESS PROCESS, I ASSURE YOU--BUT THEY'LL AWAKEN WITH ALL THE TECHNICAL KNOWLEDGE WE HAVE AT OUR DISPOSAL... ...THAT, AND ONE HELL OF A HEADACHE...

DAY THREE...
SERGEANT GOLU! THEY'RE STARTING TO COME TO...
ABOUT TIME! THIRTY-SIX HOURS IS A LONG ENOUGH ABSORPTION PERIOD! TIME TO GET THEM OUT ON THE FIELD!
OOOOOOOO! MY HEAD!

NOW WHAT, MR. CHAIRMAN?
WE WILL TEST THEM UNDER SIMULATED CIRCUMSTANCES FOR ENDURANCE, TRACKING ABILITY, REFLEXIVE THOUGHT, INTUITIVENESS--ALL THE TRAITS A CADET MUST DEMONSTRATE TO BECOME A GOOD LAWKEEPER...

THRILLING! MAY I WATCH?
MIRANDA!
OF COURSE, MY DEAR, BUT ONLY FROM THIS OBSERVATION ROOM. THE TRAINING COURSE ITSELF IS PRIMITIVE, RUGGED...AND DANGEROUS.

DANGEROUS...

IS IT TAKEN CARE OF?
THE BRIBE WAS ACCEPTED, HERR GENERAL. IT'S ALL ARRANGED...

I CANNOT CONCENTRATE--MY HEAD THROBS LIKE THE BEATING OF A THOUSAND DRUMS. GOLU SPEAKS, BUT I HEAR ONLY ONE VOICE, SEE ONLY ONE FACE--MIRANDA'S!
--MUST TRACK THE ANIMAL AND CAPTURE IT, ALIVE! EACH ONE IS TAGGED TO MATCH YOUR CADET NUMBER --YOU MUST CAPTURE YOUR ANIMAL, AND NOT YOUR OPPONENTS'.

UGLY BEASTS, BUT RELATIVELY HARMLESS. JUST BE CAREFUL OF THOSE TEETH. THEY CAN CHOMP RIGHT THROUGH A MAN'S AIRHOSE!

RELEASE THE ZABOIKS!

ATTEN-SHUN! YOU HAVE ONE HOUR EXACTLY TO TRACK AND RECOVER. ANY CADET WHO EXCEEDS THIS ONE HOUR LIMIT WILL BE ELIMINATED FROM COMPETITION.

YOU MAY BEGIN...

SILVERHEELS! MOVE IT!

THE FOOL! HA-HA-HA-HA!

SHE CALLS TO MY THOUGHTS, SHE BECKONS IN MY DREAMS. SHE KNOWS MY MIND THE WAY I KNOW THE MINDS OF OTHERS--SHE SEES INTO MY SOUL, I CANNOT ESCAPE HER...
I TRY TO TRACK, TO FIND THE CREATURE, BUT MEMORIES INVADE ME, I CANNOT FIND MY WAY...
MIRANDA...
--WAITING FOR ME? BUT YOU DIDN'T EVEN KNOW I EXISTED!
I KNEW! I SENSED IT! YOU HAD TO EXIST--FOR ME!
HER LIPS, SO COOL, SO INNOCENT--
--HER SKIN, SO SMOOTH, SO FAIR--
--HER HANDS, SO ...KNOWING...
...MIRANDA...

THERE--I FELT IT! A TINY, PRIMITIVE BURST OF THOUGHT! THE ZABOIK!

AAAGHH!

Chapter 3

--QUITE COMPLICATED, REALLY, BUT I'LL TRY TO SIMPLIFY IT FOR YOU. EACH CADET HAS A CODE--
KRAUS, FIRST IN! GOOD TIME, KRAUS...

THE CODE IS FED INTO OUR TELECOMPUTER, WHICH SCANS THE TRAINING AREA. REMARKABLE DEVICE, REALLY...
STEPPEL, SECOND. NOT BAD, STEPPEL...

REINHART, JOFFEE, STERN!
--CAN SEE THROUGH ROCK, VEGETATION, EVEN ANIMAL MATTER IF SO INDICATED. EACH CADET CAN BE LOCATED AT A MOMENT'S NOTICE--

--THERE'S YOUR FIANCE, MY DEAR--
MAY I TRY?
FEDDERS, HIMMEL, YOU'RE DRAGGING, BOYS!
WHO'S LEFT?
SILVERHEELS, SIR!

ONLY TEN MINUTES LEFT... SILVERHEELS!
...SILVERHEELS...

SILVERHEELS!

OH MY--!
GET ME SERGEANT GOLU, QUICKLY!
--QUADRANE 74, RIGHT!
KRAUS, REINHART, COME WITH ME!
IT'S STRANGLING HIM!
--JUST IN TIME TO RECOVER THE REMAINS! HA-HA!

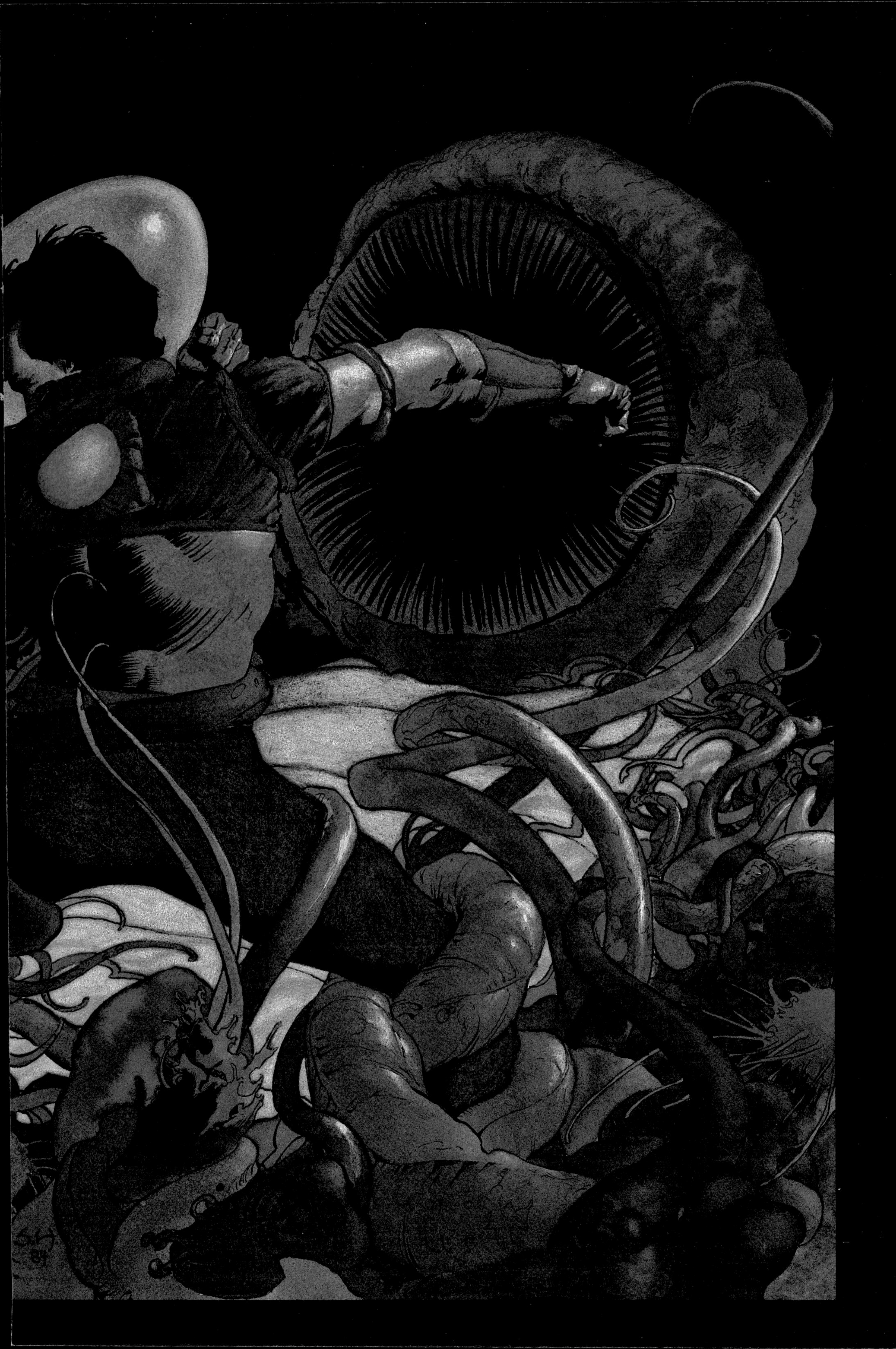

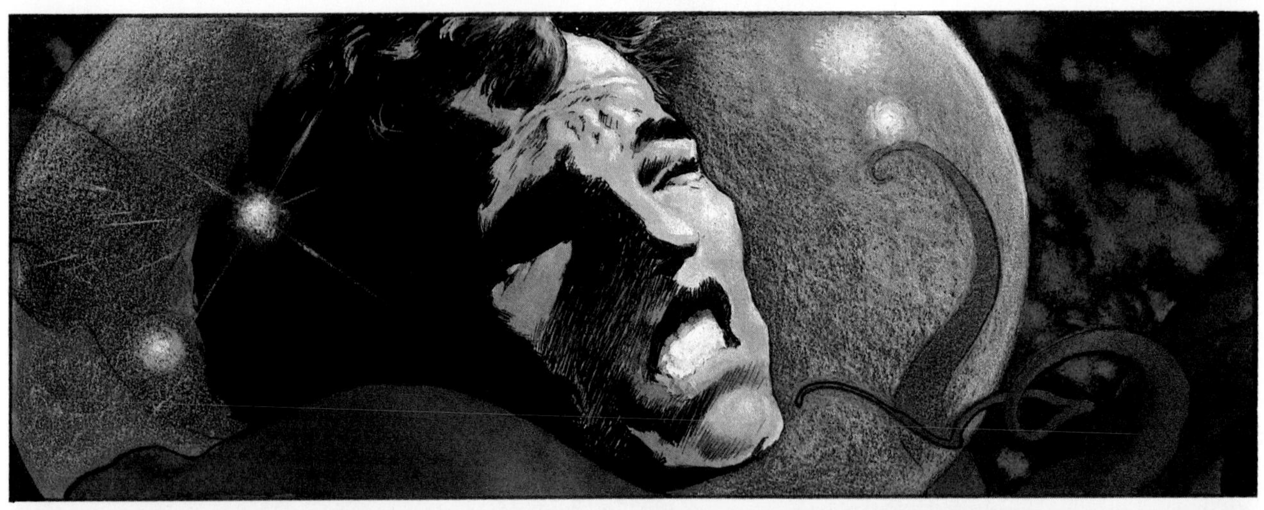

YOU MUST THRUST AT THE HEART OF THE BEAST, MY SON--FOR WITH-IN THE HEART ALL THE SECRETS OF THE LIFE-FORCE RESIDE...

AAANEEE!
THIS WAY!
MY ZABOIK, SIR...
...WITH A MINUTE TO SPARE...
BUT SIR, HE USED A NON-REGULATION WEAPON, HE--
SHUT UP, KRAUS.
GOOD WORK, SON...
...SILVERHEELS...

--HIS METHODS WERE UNCONVENTIONAL, SIR, I ADMIT, BUT THIS BOY'S GOT SOME-THING--
I'M NOT INTERESTED IN HIS METHODS, SERGEANT. I WANT TO KNOW HOW THAT CREATURE GOT INTO THE TRAINING ZONE!
I--DON'T KNOW, SIR...
WHAT'S HAPPENED TO SECURITY AROUND HERE? IT'S BECOME TOO LAX FOR MY TASTES! FROM NOW ON EVERYONE IS CON-FINED TO QUARTERS AFTER 0600. AND I DO MEAN EVERY-ONE!

AND SERGEANT, I WANT SPECIAL GUARDS ASSIGNED TO THE GENERAL AND HIS DAUGHTER--
--THERE'S SOMETHING ABOUT HER I DON'T TRUST--
MIRANDA, MY DARLING, WHAT A WONDERFUL SURPRISE!
(GASP!) STEPAN!
LET GO OF ME, YOU FOOL!

IS THAT ANY WAY TO SPEAK TO YOUR FIANCE, MY LOVE?
I'M NOT YOUR LOVE! WE WERE MATCHED BY COMPUTER, NOT PASSION! YOU MAKE MY SKIN CRAWL!
YOU PREFER THAT DIRTY RED, I SUPPOSE!
WHAT OF IT? WE'RE NOT MARRIED YET!
ENJOY HIM WHILE YOU MAY, MY LOVE. HE'S NOT LONG FOR THIS LIFE...
WHAT DO YOU MEAN?
WAIT. YOU'LL FIND OUT.
YOU KNOW, MIRANDA, YOU'RE AN ENIGMA. THE PERFECT NAZITE FEMALE, PHYSICALLY, BUT YOUR PRINCIPLES ARE WARPED, CORRUPT. YOU REMIND ME, IN FACT, OF MY OWN FATHER--
--AND YOU KNOW WHAT HAPPENED TO HIM...

Chapter 4

YOU DARE TO THREATEN *ME*? THE *GENERAL'S DAUGHTER*?
AND *MY MATE!* DON'T FORGET! ONCE WE'RE MARRIED YOU'LL DO *MY WILL*, OR I'LL TAKE IT OUT ON YOUR SOFT WHITE FLESH!

AGH!

YOU *BITCH!* I'LL KILL --
KRAUS, WHAT'S GOING ON HERE?
NOTHING ...SIR...
BACK TO THE BARRACKS! AND YOU, MISS-- I MUST INSIST YOU RETURN TO YOUR QUARTERS AND STAY THERE UNTIL MORNING.
IF YOU SAY SO, SERGEANT...

DAY 5...
USUALLY AT THIS JUNCTURE WE SEND THE CADETS TO COURSE 3 FOR ENDURANCE TESTING -- HOWEVER...
SERGEANT GOLU HAS SUGGESTED AN ALTERNATIVE WHICH WILL TEST COURAGE AND LOYALTY TO THE LAWKEEPERS' CODE AS WELL...
SERGEANT GOLU, IF YOU PLEASE...
THANK YOU, MR. CHAIRMAN ...LISTEN UP, CADETS! EACH OF YOU WILL BE PAIRED WITH ANOTHER CADET FOR COMBAT TRAINING IN THE "HOT HOUSE"...
YOU WILL BE ATTACKED FROM ALL SIDES, BUT REMEMBER--YOUR DUTY IS TO PROTECT YOUR PARTNER! ANY CADET WHO FAILS TO DO SO WILL BE INSTANTLY ELIMINATED FROM COMPETITION.
OKAY, HERE'S THE LINE-UP! REINHART WITH STEPPEL, HIMMEL WITH STERN, JOFFEE WITH FEDDERS--
AND KRAUS WITH SILVERHEELS!
GASP!
REPORT TO THE TAKE-OFF PAD ON LAUNCH 6 TO AWAIT FURTHER INSTRUCTIONS! DISMISSED! THAT MEANS YOU, SILVERHEELS!

WE CALL THIS THE "HOT HOUSE." YOU'LL UNDERSTAND WHY IN A MINUTE. EACH TEAM WILL BE DROPPED IN A DIFFERENT SECTOR. ALL YOU HAVE TO DO IS SURVIVE...

...WHICH, I GUARANTEE, WON'T BE EASY...

REMEMBER, PROTECT YOUR PARTNER! WHATEVER THE COST! OTHERWISE YOU'RE OUT!
GOOD LUCK-- YOU'LL NEED IT!

KA-POW!
"PROTECT YOUR PARTNER." ISN'T THAT WHAT HE SAID?
NO THANKS IS REQUIRED...
NONE'S GIVEN! I'D SOONER BE DEAD THAN SAVED BY YOU!
DON'T WORRY, LITTLE RED. THAT WILL BE ARRANGED --LATER.

"WE SET UP CAMP AND WAITED FOR NIGHTFALL. OF COURSE, I DO THIS WELL. KRAUS IS AWKWARD-- HIS LIFE IS THE GLEAMING CITY, NOT THE FOREST. BUT NONE CAN BEAT HIM WITH A LASERGUN..."
WATCH THIS, LITTLE RED!

KA-CHOW

PLOP

A GIFT FOR MY PARTNER!
...I'M NOT HUNGRY...

SUIT YOURSELF! BUT THE NIGHT IS LONG AND OUR RATIONS ARE SHORT--
AND YOUR CHATTER IS BORING, KRAUS. KEEP IT TO YOURSELF!

SUPPOSE THIS WERE YOUR HEAD, SILVERHEELS... I WONDER IF YOU'D BE SO IMPUDENT THEN...
...OR WOULD YOU SCREAM AS I FLAYED YOU ALIVE?

...PERHAPS WE'LL NEVER KNOW! SWEET DREAMS, LITTLE RED!
HA-HA-HA-HA-HA-HA!

"THE NIGHT IS FALSE, MANUFACTURED BY THEIR TECHNOLOGY, BUT I WELCOME IT ALL THE SAME. IF I CAN'T SEE MIRANDA BY DAY, I WILL SEARCH FOR HER IN MY DREAMS. I SHUT MY EYES AND--"
AAHHEEE
KRAUS? WHAT IS IT? KRAUS?
...BE-BEHIND YOU...

WHO ARE YOU? WHAT DO YOU WANT?

OOMPH!

NOW WE'RE EVEN...

"HIS INJURIES WERE SLIGHT--"

"--EXCEPT ONE--"
YOUR NECK, KRAUS! YOU'VE BEEN SCRATCHED BY THE MONSTER!

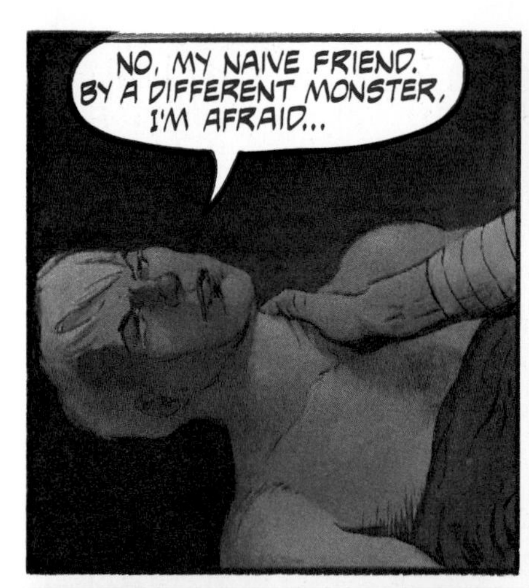
NO, MY NAIVE FRIEND. BY A DIFFERENT MONSTER, I'M AFRAID...

MIRANDA!
YES, MIRANDA, MY DELICATE, LOYAL FIANCÉE!

DID SHE TELL YOU SHE'D BEEN WAITING FOR YOU ALL HER LIFE? FOOL SHE'D HAD EVERY MAN IN THE BARRACKS BY THE TIME SHE WAS FIFTEEN! INCLUDING ME!
LIAR! I DON'T BELIEVE YOU!

OH, YOU BELIEVE ME, ALL RIGHT. I CAN SEE IT IN YOUR EYES...
IF YOU DIDN'T, YOU'D KILL ME ON THE SPOT, TO SAVE HER HONOR. THAT'S THE 'PACHEE CODE, ISN'T IT?
WELL, LITTLE RED... NOW'S YOUR CHANCE...

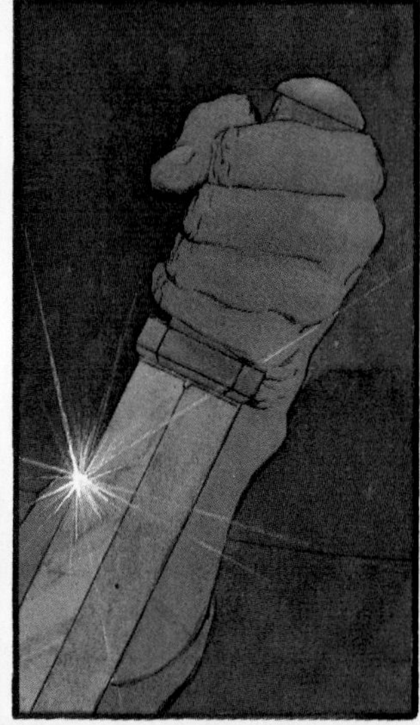

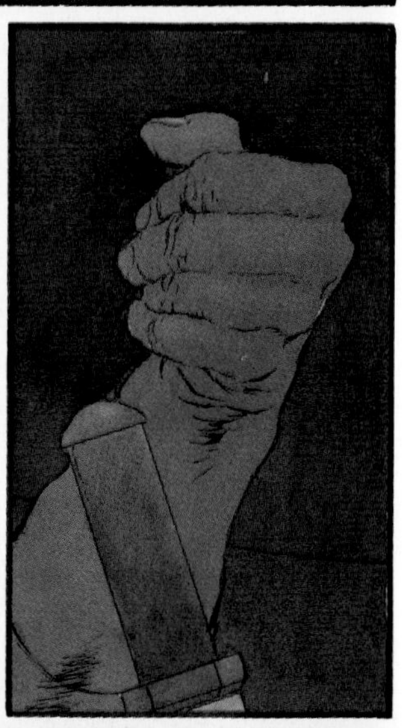

...YOU'RE NOT THE FIRST TO BE FOOLED ...NOR WILL YOU BE THE LAST...

"FOR THREE DAYS WE FOUGHT THE JUNGLE-- KRAUS RECOVERED FROM HIS WOUNDS, FOR THEY WERE MERELY PHYSICAL. WOUNDS OF THE HEART ARE ANOTHER MATTER..."
LOOK, THERE'S STERN! HEY, STERN!
SAVE YOUR BREATH, KRAUS. HE'S DEAD...
IT WASN'T MY FAULT, KRAUS! IT WAS HIM OR ME!
IT WAS A MONSTER, KRAUS! TWENTY FEET LONG, WITH STINGERS! IT WAS *HORRIBLE, HORRIBLE!*
SNIVELLING COWARD! YOU WERE SUPPOSED TO PROTECT HIM! NOW YOU'LL BE ELIMINATED FROM THE PROGRAM!
BUT I'M ALIVE! AND YOU KNOW AS WELL AS I THAT I DIDN'T STAND A CHANCE, ANYWAY-- YOU WERE THE ONE WHO WAS CHOSEN TO--
SHUT YOUR STUPID MOUTH, HIMMEL, OR I'LL--

--MEIN GOTT!!
NOOOo!

HELP ME! HELP ME!
KKRREEM!

THIS IS NO MACHINE! IT'S FLESH AND BLOOD!

YOUR NOBLE FEDERATION! SO CONCERNED WITH PRESERVING LIFE!
IT DID A VERY POOR JOB OF PRESERVING HIMMEL'S...

IF REINHART'S DEAD, THEN STEPPEL MUST BE, TOO. THAT LEAVES ONLY US, MY LITTLE FRIEND...THE FEDERATION'S KILLED THE REST. WHY DON'T YOU USE THOSE SPECIAL POWERS OF YOURS TO SEE WHAT THEY HAVE IN STORE FOR US? PER-HAPS WE'LL BE EATEN BY A GIANT MILLIPEDE, OR ROASTED ALIVE IN A VOLCANO!

"BUT KRAUS WAS RIGHT, UNCANNILY RIGHT. HE SEEMED TO KNOW MY MIND BETTER THAN I KNEW IT MYSELF. MY OBSESSION WITH MIRANDA HAD DESTROYED MY GIFT. WITHOUT IT, WITHOUT HER, I HAD NOTHING TO LIVE FOR..."

COME ON, YOU RED BASTARD!

NO!

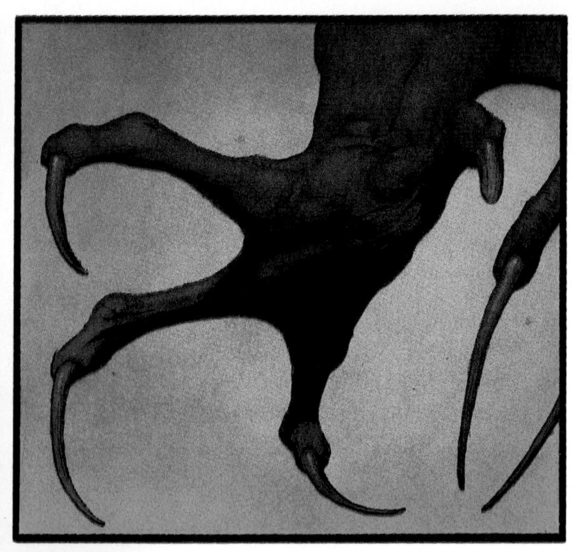

AAAAAIIIIIEEEEEEEEEEE

SILVERHEELS!!

ZZZZZTTT
...YOU SAVED ME...YOU SAVED ME...
...THANK YOU... SILVER-HEELS...

HE'S BACK!

IT'S OVER, SILVERHEELS.
...WHAT...I... WHERE AM I?
REINHART! BUT YOU'RE DEAD!
NOT DEAD, SILVERHEELS, ONLY ELIMINATED FROM COMPETITION. YOU DIDN'T THINK WE'D LET ANY OF YOU DIE, NOW DID YOU?

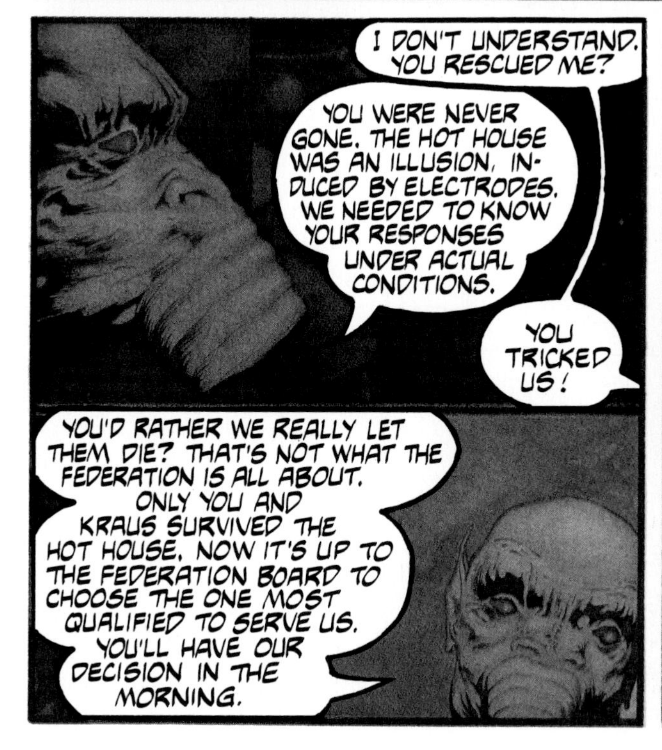
I DON'T UNDERSTAND. YOU RESCUED ME?
YOU WERE NEVER GONE. THE HOT HOUSE WAS AN ILLUSION, INDUCED BY ELECTRODES. WE NEEDED TO KNOW YOUR RESPONSES UNDER ACTUAL CONDITIONS.
YOU TRICKED US!
YOU'D RATHER WE REALLY LET THEM DIE? THAT'S NOT WHAT THE FEDERATION IS ALL ABOUT. ONLY YOU AND KRAUS SURVIVED THE HOT HOUSE. NOW IT'S UP TO THE FEDERATION BOARD TO CHOOSE THE ONE MOST QUALIFIED TO SERVE US. YOU'LL HAVE OUR DECISION IN THE MORNING.

IN THE MEANTIME, I THINK THERE IS SOMEONE WHO WISHES TO SEE YOU...COME, MEN...

SILVERHEELS!

BUT... WHAT'S WRONG? DON'T YOU LOVE ME?
KRAUS TOLD ME ABOUT YOU--HOW YOU EAT MEN'S HEARTS LIKE A HUNGRY ANIMAL...
THE 'PACHEES HAVE A SAYING: "FAY VILLI, SEIGI ELL'N VO..." "WITHOUT TRUST, THERE IS NO LOVE..." I NO LONGER TRUST YOU.

YOU DON'T TRUST ME, BUT YOU TRUST KRAUS, YOUR WORST ENEMY, A MAN WHO BETRAYED HIS OWN FATHER FOR SLEEPING WITH A 'PACHEE WOMAN!
...I ADMIT, MY LOVE, I'VE BEEN EVIL ALL MY LIFE... BUT I'VE NEVER LIED TO YOU ...AND I NEVER SHALL...

ELSEWHERE--
WHAT DO YOU MEAN, YOU REFUSE!?! IF THE FEDERATION CHOOSES SILVERHEELS INSTEAD OF YOU, WE'RE FINISHED!

HE SAVED MY LIFE...
NONSENSE! IT WASN'T EVEN REAL!
HE THOUGHT IT WAS... I SEEM LINKED TO HIM SOMEHOW... SOME WAY...

THE SON OF A TRAITOR BECOMES A TRAITOR HIMSELF! I MIGHT HAVE KNOWN! YOU'D BETTER PRAY TO THAT 'PACHEE'S HEATHEN GOD THAT THE FEDERATION CHOOSES YOU TOMORROW--
--FOR YOU'LL NEVER RETURN TO EARTH ALIVE... I'LL SEE TO THAT!

THAT NIGHT...
SILVERHEELS...
MY SON...
GRANDFERE! AM I DREAMING?

MY POWERS! THEY'RE BACK!
MY SON, LISTEN. THE TIME HAS COME FOR YOU TO KNOW...

"YOUR MOTHER DID NOT DIE IN CHILDBIRTH. THE 'PACHEES KILLED HER--"

"--FOR CONSORTING WITH A WHITE MAN! YOU SEE, YOU ARE THE SON OF A NAZITE!"

THE NAZITE WAS ALSO KILLED, BETRAYED BY HIS OWN SMALL SON.
...GRANDFERE... WHAT WAS MY FATHER'S NAME?...

"BUT I KNEW THE ANSWER BEFORE IT CAME..."
KRAUS... JOSEPH KRAUS...

...KRAUS! ...STEPAN KRAUS!

CONGRATULATIONS, KRAUS!
THANK YOU, SIR...

AND, FOR THE FIRST TIME IN THE HISTORY OF THE ACADEMY, WE HAVE A TIE. WE ARE AWARDING THE POSITION OF YOUR PARTNER TO --SILVERHEELS!

NOW WE TRULY *ARE* PARTNERS!
MORE THAN PARTNERS, KRAUS... FRIENDS...

WE IN THE FEDERATION HAVE FOUND THAT THERE IS ONE CONSTANT IN THE UNIVERSE-- THE CAPACITY FOR GROWTH IN THE HUMAN SPIRIT. BOTH OF YOU HAVE EVIDENCED THAT CAPACITY, AND WILL CONTINUE TO GROW THROUGH YOUR PARTNERSHIP...
I SALUTE YOU!

COME, MIRANDA! OUR FATE IS SEALED --WE MUST ESCAPE!
NO, FATHER. THE CHAIRMAN HAS CON-SENTED TO LET ME STAY ON HERE AND SERVE THE FED-ERATION!
MY OWN DAUGHTER, FALL-ING VICTIM TO THAT DIRTY RED! FILTH!

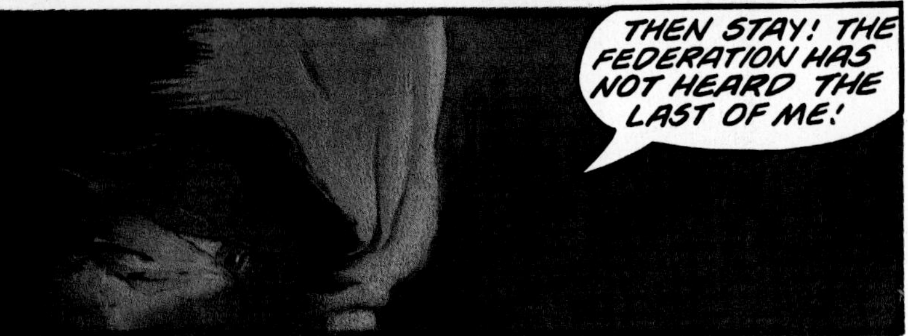
THEN STAY! THE FEDERATION HAS NOT HEARD THE LAST OF ME!

"WE'VE BEEN IN SPACE THREE MONTHS NOW, KRAUS AND I. I HAVEN'T TOLD HIM MY *SECRET*-- PERHAPS I NEVER SHALL. BUT THERE ARE TIMES WHEN WE SEEM TO *SHARE* ONE MIND, ONE HEART--

--AND ONE LOVE FOR ONE WOMAN. I DON'T KNOW IF I'LL EVER SEE MIRANDA AGAIN, I DON'T KNOW IF I EVER WANT TO.

"--'***FAY VILLI, SEIGI ELL'N VO***'... I TOLD HER... 'WITHOUT TRUST, THERE IS NO LOVE'..." BUT HER LAST WORDS PLAY IN MY MIND OVER AND OVER AGAIN--"

The Eclipse Graphic Album Series:
Sabre by Don McGregor and Paul Gulacy
Night Music by P. Craig Russell
Detectives, Inc. by Don McGregor and Marshall Rogers
Stewart the Rat by Steve Gerber,
Gene Colan and Tom Palmer
The Price by Jim Starlin
I Am Coyote by Steve Englehart and Marshall Rogers
The Rocketeer by Dave Stevens
Zorro by Nedaud and Marcello
The Sacred and the Profane by Ken Steacy and Dean Motler
Somerset Holmes by Bruce Jones, April Campbell and Brent Anderson
Floyd Farland by Chris Ware